Diary of a Valiant Wolf

Book 1: Steve's Wolves

Mark Mulle

DEDICATION

This book is dedicated to all Minecraft lovers.

CONTENTS

Day 1

Hello! My name is Boris. I am a Minecraft wolf. I have a lovely wife and two cute cubs. We live a happy and healthy life in this world of blocks! We have a lot of fun in our daily routines surviving on our own, finding food, and avoiding the night creatures.

Despite our peaceful lives, I've noticed weird things going on in this world recently. Huge holes on the dirt, strange caves appearing in the mountains, floating trees without any wood on them, and even entire rivers disappearing from their course. As the leader of my pack, it is my duty to find out what's happening, and what or who is causing this disturbance. We live inside a big cave near a river.

Day 2

Today, I took my cubs to the woods. I wanted to teach them some valuable lessons to grow up to be strong and smart wolves. With the recent strange occurrences, I want them to learn how to protect themselves and face any threats they might run into.

But they're still too young... We'll have to start from the very beginning. The basics of being a wolf are simple: First, you must find food (sheep). Second, you must find a safe place to stay at night to avoid the monsters. And third, you must learn how to swim. Because, why not? There's so much water around this place that it's a very important survival skill. They're quick learners, and I believe this won't take too long.

Day 3

Another day of hard training. They're doing great! Tasha is very smart and she can spot a sheep from miles away, but she's terrified of the water. I must teach her how to swim and lose her fear of the water. Lobo, on the other hand, is an avid swimmer but his survival instincts for finding food are not really good… I'll have to focus on different aspects of each one of them from now on. My best bet is to teach them individually, but I'm really proud to see how smart they are.

Day 4

Today, during our daily training in the middle of the woods, we saw a huge storm approaching. I had never seen anything like it with huge and dark clouds above our heads. I told Tasha and Lobo to stop with their exercises, because we'd have to continue another day. I asked them to follow me; we had to leave the woods immediately. Fortunately, we weren't really far from our cave, and we got there just in time. Their mother was extremely worried about us, but we were safe and sound. During the storm, I noticed something really weird, far from our cave: a very bright light, shining from the woods in the distance. I have no idea what that is, but I definitely want to find out as soon as this storm is gone.

Day 5

On the morning following the storm, I got up early and left the cave. I wanted to explore that strange place before taking my kids to their training. I told my wife Susi to wait for me there. I left the cave and headed towards the bright light from the other night. I couldn't see anything other than trees and blocks, but I knew there was something hiding in there. Something new and mysterious. That bright light could be the origin of that huge storm, because I had never seen it there before.

Upon arriving at the strange place, I must confess I was a bit scared. Even though I'm a strong and valiant wolf, that place was very creepy and weird. It was a box made of wood. I still wonder what kind of creature could have made a box like that. This box was very tall and large, as if someone had gathered a lot of different wooden blocks and put them together. What kind of trick is that? I know the Endermen can carry blocks and whatnot, but this is nonsense! I doubt they had anything to do with that box. I had to return to my cave and tell my wife about the box. But then, I saw something inside the box...

A tall creature, standing on its two feet, using some sort of cloth over its body. I'd never seen that creature around, and I have been living here for a long time! But what really caught my attention was that the creature was being followed around... by a wolf! But this wolf was different, he had a red thing around his neck, and he would obey the creature's orders. Is that some sort of sorcery? Why is the wolf following that thing? I had to stay a bit longer... and wait for them to come outside. I'll try to convince this wolf to run away from this place with me, let me see if I can save that poor creature from his prison.

Day 6

I waited for many, many hours. Eventually, I felt asleep because I was very tired after staying over a day without any sleep. Luckily I was behind a tree, where they couldn't see me! I just woke up, and it's around noon. And they're still inside... I guess I should find something to eat while I wait for them to come out.

From what I can see, it seems the wolf serves as the creature's bodyguard. He's very loyal and follows him around. The tall creature possesses a great power: he can control blocks and place them anywhere he wants. He can also create different objects made of blocks. It's amazing, but I have no idea what he wants to do with such power?

Day 7

I waited for the entire day. They wouldn't leave the box. The tall creature was so busy creating new objects and placing them around, and the wolf would just stay there without doing anything.

It was very late at night when they finally left their hut for the first time in three days. The creature went out first and started building something with his bare hands a few feet from the hut. The wolf was right behind him. I approached the wolf carefully and touched him with my paws. I whispered:

- "Hey, I'm here to help you, let's get out of here now!"

He didn't say a word. He stood still, didn't even look at me! I tried again.

- "C'mon, we gotta get going! I live inside a small cave with my family not far from here, I can take you there!"

Nothing. This time, I pushed him a few times, and then he attacked me out of nowhere! I had to leave because the creature saw me there too. I ran away as fast as I could and after fleeing, I hid behind a big tree to catch my breath. What's going on here? Why is the wolf so violent towards other wolves? He must be out of his mind. I just can't leave him there... even if he doesn't want me around.

Day 8

I was about to get home after my failed attempt to talk with the wolf. I was still impressed by that amazing creature standing on its feet, and the wolf following him. I have so many questions right now… I really need to find out why the wolf lives with that creature.

I can't go back home just yet, I can't give up on that wolf; he could be in danger! I guess I'll sleep by the trees and give it another try tomorrow.

Day 9

I had to give it another try. After spending the night in the woods, I returned to their place. After getting there, I saw the wolf and the creature outside. That was my chance to reach the wolf. I waited for the creature to return to his hut. When he did, I jumped on the wolf and told him:

- "Hey, what's wrong with you? Why did you attack me? Let's get out of here!" I was expecting him to attack me again, but I was prepared now. Instead, he said:

- "No, I don't want to leave".

- "Wh… What? Are you nuts? Why do you want to stay?" I asked him.

- "Look, I'm sorry for attacking you like that. But I won't leave Steve."

- "Steve… That creature's name is Steve? Why do you want to stay with him?"

- "I'll explain later; Come back here in two days. I have to go."

And he simply disappeared. Just like that! I looked inside the hut, and no one was there. Not even the creature called Steve. Things are getting really weird here, but I'll return because I want to hear his story, his explanation.

Day 10

After I returned home, my wife and kids were really worried about me. I had been out for a few days, but I explained everything. I told them the story of the mysterious wolf living with a creature called Steve. I told them how powerful Steve was, and how the wolf attacked me and preferred to stay with Steve instead of running away with me. They were super confused at first, just like me. But I told them of my plan to return there. My wife asked me to stay home... she doesn't want me to meddle with that weird creature, but I must know what's going on behind that wolf's story! She agreed after a while. We went to sleep early because I was really tired.

Day 11

I woke up early in the morning. I wanted to take Tasha and Lobo for a long day of training before leaving to visit the wolf in the hut, because they haven't trained at all in days. They were really out of shape, so we mostly had fun chasing a few sheep and swimming by the river. After a nice day with my cubs, I took them back to the cave. I kissed everyone and wished them a good night of sleep. I promised I'd be back from my adventure as soon as I could, and I'd do my best to bring the wolf with me. I asked Susi to look after the kids, and told them to continue with their training. I left the cave and headed towards the strange hut to meet the wolf.

Day 12

I waited there for many hours… It was dark and I was right in front of the hut. I thought the wolf had forgotten about our meeting, but suddenly I heard a small noise coming from the hut. The wolf was there.

- "Oh, hello! Good to see you came."

- "Uh, hi. Yeah, well… I really want to take you out of this prison".

- "Hahaha, you're so silly! This is not a prison of any sort, buddy. This is my house! It's where I live". He was so confident of what he was saying;

- "Your… house? What do you mean? What about that creature, Steve? Who is that?"

- "Steve is my owner. We look after each other, and we live here together"

- "I didn't know we could have owners… But why? Isn't it better to live in the woods, just like any other wolf?"

He looked at me for a few seconds, and said "I don't think so… The life out there is extremely dangerous. Many monsters come out at night, and we have to look for food every day. It's a harsh life and I have everything I want right here!"

- "I see… But, why did you attack me?"

- "Haha sorry about that! You see, Steve is looking for more wolves to live here with us. And once you become Steve's wolf, you can't go back. You mentioned having a family, and I think you should consider talking with them about this first; they might want to come here with you!"

- "I… I'll have to think about it. Let me talk to the others, and I'll get back to you. Oh, uh, one more thing? You DISAPPEARED in front of me. How did you do that?"

- "Ah, yes! It's an ability you get once Steve tames you. It allows you to teleport to him at anytime, whenever you want. It's very useful to protect Steve in tough situations."

- Okay, I guess. I'll get back in a few days."

Day 13

My attempts to convince this wolf of coming home with me have failed. I could not take him out of there, and had to return home on my own. After arriving at the cave, I found my wife and kids there. They were really happy to see me. Susi asked me about the other wolf, and I told her the whole story. She listened to me carefully without saying a word. After finishing the story, she looked at me and said:

- "Boris... Just think about that for a moment. That sounds like a very good opportunity, don't you think? Living a better, safer life and not having to worry about anything else..."

- "What are you talking about, Susi? We have a perfectly safe life here!"

- "Inside a cave? I don't think so, Boris. Please, just tell me you'll think about it. We could go there and meet this Steve guy you've been talking about, why don't we give him a chance? From what you said, this place sounds like a good place for us."

- "Okay... What about this? I'll take all of you there to have a look, and then you tell me what you think about the place. I'm sure you won't like it! That guy lives in a tiny box made of wood and sand; it's weird and ugly!"

Day 14

My wife's crazy… She wants to live in a box with Steve and his wolf! That box doesn't look comfortable at all, and I bet all of the night monsters can get inside easily. She'll definitely change her mind once we get there and see it for herself: haha, I bet! The kids are super happy to travel to a different place at least, for once, and they're planning everything today. We'll travel tomorrow in the morning.

Day 15

This is the big day. We're going to visit Steve and his wolf. Oh in hindsight, I've never asked for his name. I guess I'll just call him Steve's wolf then... Anyway, on our way to the hut, the kids wouldn't stop talking. They were super excited to get there and see the box with their own eyes. "A box made of piled blocks? That's impossible!" they said. "You'll see it kids, but trust me – there's nothing interesting in that box. "

After walking for a few hours, we got there. But to my surprise, the place was different. In fact, everything was extremely different, even the box. Wait, that's not the box I saw on that first day. This box was much, much bigger. No, it's huge! Oh my, how did this happen? I knew the Steve guy can pile up blocks and stuff, but this?! My wife stared at me for a while, and said, "tiny box of wood, huh?"

- "But, but... Trust me; the box was smaller than this! A LOT smaller! It was super tiny and..."

- "Okay, okay, no problem, honey. But where's that wolf and his guy?"

We looked around, but there was no one. Suddenly, there was a huge noise: a big hole opened up right in front of the big box. It was him, the Steve guy! He came out of the box directly towards us. I thought he was going to attack us, but then he said:

- "Oh great, more wolves! I've been looking for you guys for many days. Come on in!"

Weird... we can understand him? That's news to me. Looking at him now, he doesn't look so scary as I thought... I think we can trust him after all.

We went inside the box, and it was even bigger than the outside. I was wrong again – the place seemed to be very comfortable and safe.

It had some pretty pictures and flowers, and other stuff hanging around and on the floor, the Steve guy knew how to create some nifty objects.

He closed the door behind us and grabbed a small box next to the door. He opened it and retrieved a few bones and fed us with them. Oh my gosh, bones! They're our favorite! But they're super hard to get, because we must defeat that Skeleton monster to grab one. We couldn't believe our eyes, that this guy had a box full of them!

- "There there, eat as many bones as you want. I need to tame you guys!"

After eating a few bones, I noticed Susi and the kids had the same red collar as the lone wolf. And so did I! The red collars appeared after we ate the bones given to us by Steve. But instead of feeling scared because of the collar, I felt really nice. As if I was safe from everything and everyone. It was a very good feeling, and my wife and kids seemed happy as well! What is this supposed to mean?

Day 16

We spent most of the day at Steve's hut (or should I call it, HUGE hut) eating bones and walking around the place. It was really big, and he even made us a special place to sleep. I must confess that this place was much better than our dark, cold cave. I believe Susi was right after all, and it was a good decision to come here. But... where's the wolf? I haven't seen him yet.

We were taking a nap right next to Steve when the wolf appeared.

- "Oopa! There you are. Where have you been, buddy? We have new guests!"

Ohh, so his name was Oopa... The more you know! I got up and smiled at Oopa, as it was nice to see him again. I introduced him to my wife and kids:

- "Susi, Tasha, and Lobo, this is Oopa, the guy who convinced you all to come here. And these are my wife and kids, Oopa!"

- "It's great to meet you guys! Welcome to Steve's castle!"

Everyone greeted him, and I had to ask.

- "Ca... castle? What's that?"

Oopa laughed.

- "It's the place we're in, silly! Steve built this huge castle from scratch, using rocks and stone."

- "Oh, I see. I used to call it a hut... but hey, can't Steve listen to us? Because I can understand him just fine."

- "No, unfortunately Steve does not understand our language, even though we can understand his. But don't worry; he's very smart and he'll take care of us if we return the favor."

20

- "So tell me, Oopa, what do we do here? Are we supposed to work as Steve's guards?" Susi asked him.

- "Yes, sort of. We must do our best to protect Steve, and he'll look after us as well. But you'll have to train in order to become good guards! I can give you guys a few lessons tomorrow if you want."

- "Huh, that would be great, thanks! I have never been a guard before, but I believe it shouldn't be that hard. Boris and I have some nice hunting skills which could come in handy!" Susi was very happy and confident.

Day 17

On the next day, Oopa woke me up very early. He told me we had to follow Steve to his mine. Well, if our duty here was to work as guards, I'd do my best to help!

We followed Steve as he walked into a big cave. But this was no regular cave. Apparently, it was carved out by Steve himself, because everything was so organized, with many torches lighting up the place. We went down and followed Steve as he dug around, using weird objects.

- "So... tell me Oopa, how long have you been here with Steve?"

- "Not long, really. Steve found me a few months ago in the woods during the night. I was running away from Zombies, and he slayed 'em all and saved me! That's why I intend to protect him for as long as I can now."

- "Oh, that's awesome! But...what about your family? Don't you have kids, wife, or parents?"

- "No, I lived most of my life all by myself. I don't have any memories of my parents and I never found another female wolf. But I believe the right day will come!"

- "Of course it will! We'll find a female wolf for you in no time. Oh, one more question... The first day I found out about the place, I saw a bright light coming out of the woods. What was that?"

- "A bright light? I believe it was Steve's Beacon. It's a structure he uses to enchant his weapons and armor."

- "I have no idea what those words mean, but I suppose it's for a greater good!"

Oopa laughed.

- "Oh look, Steve's taken all of the ores he needed. We're heading back home!"

Day 18

On the next day, Steve spent most of his time inside the castle. He would craft stuff and place objects on the floor. I thought it would be a good idea to take my family for a walk. There's a big river behind the castle, and I took Susi, Tasha and Lobo there to have some fun. I invited Oopa to join us, but he wanted to stay there in case Steve needed him.

It was a very nice day; the kids had a blast playing in the river. Susi and I laughed a lot, watching our kids play in the river. It's great to live here; I'll do my best to help Steve defeat the Dragon and keep the night creatures away from our home!

Day 19

Our new life in this new castle is very good. We follow Steve and make sure he doesn't get attacked by the night creatures. But since those monsters don't come out during the day, we don't have a lot of work to do. My kids spend most of their time playing around, having fun inside the castle and playing outside. They're still practicing the skills I taught them: there's a river nearby, and they swim there often. They also hunt sheep and bring some of their wool in every once in a while. Susi takes care of the kids but sometimes, she also comes with us to protect Steve.

Life here is so peaceful and calm... I still wonder why Steve needs so many wolves to protect him? I'm curious to know what he's planning to do.

Day 20

Today, we followed Steve into the mine again, just Oopa and me. We spent many hours down there, and I asked Oopa about Steve's plans for the future.

- "So, Oopa. I see Steve is coming down here quite often... What exactly is he doing?"

- "He's gathering some ores to craft better tools and weapons, and a better armor. He needs a lot of diamonds to get the best tier."

- "Diamonds are those blue gems? Okay, makes sense. But tell me, why does he need us after all? Apparently he can take care of himself just fine."

- "Steve wants to defeat a big creature known as the Ender Dragon. This dragon lives in another dimension called The End. The dragon is the reason why so many monsters spawn during the night."

- "Oh really? That's interesting. But does it mean we're going with him to defeat this dragon creature?"

- "No, we can't. Only Steve can get inside the realm, and he's the only one who can defeat the monster. Our job here is to protect Steve in this world. I know we haven't had a lot to do so far, but trust me, we will and soon! Steve is going to pay a visit to a village priest in a few days, to ask him about The End's location. We'll go with him to make sure everything goes as intended."

- "Nice. I'll do my best to protect Steve, then! He must defeat the dragon to get rid of the night monsters."

- "That's the spirit! I'm sure we'll do a very good job."

Day 21

Today was another normal day. We followed Steve into the mine; he's been mining a lot lately to get more ores and craft new stuff. He also spent some of his time in the world above, hunting a few animals to get food. It was fun putting my hunting skills to the test again; Susi and I chased some pigs and cows around, and Oopa was very impressed with our skills. We had a feast tonight, with lots of meat for everyone! Life's been very good, but I'm also looking forward to our trip to the village that Oopa was talking about.

Day 22

I was in a deep sleep when something awoke me.

- "Boris, get up! C'mon, we have to go!"

- "Ugh… What's… Going on?"

- "Let's go Boris, Steve is leaving right now. We're going to the village, and we need to leave as soon as possible!"

- "Ah, okay. I'll be ready in a minute."

So today was the day! I knew Oopa said we'd leave 'soon', but I didn't know it would be THIS soon. I asked Susi to stay there with the kids as they couldn't come with us because it could be dangerous, but I promised her we'd get back soon.

Steve was outside. Oopa and I followed him. He knelt before us and said:

- "Alright, boys! We're going to the village today. It's gonna be a long trip, but if we work as a team everything's gonna be fine! Now, let's get going."

Steve was very confident, and so were we. I was super anxious to go, because I have never been to a village before. What was it like? Who are we going to meet? Does he really know how to defeat the dragon? I know I'm not the savior of the world here, but I really wanna know everything!

Day 23

What a long day. We just walked, and walked, and walked again. I can barely feel my paws right now! We traveled so much that, I have no idea how far we are from the castle. We walked by deserts, forests, rivers, and snowy mountains. Now we're sleeping inside a cave (something I'm used to) and we'll depart early in the morning. Steve said the village is not far now. I hope he's right!

Day 24

Another long day. We walked the entire morning and stopped for a few minutes to get something to eat. After having our lunch, we continued. But when I thought we still had a long journey ahead of us, Oopa spotted something on the horizon.

- "Look, Boris! It's the village!"

And he was right. At first, we could only see a small tower. But as we crossed the small forest we were in, we saw more houses and many weird creatures walking around. So that's what a village looks like.

- "That's awesome! We're finally going to meet the priest!" I said.

- "Steve must be really excited to meet him as well."

When we finally got there, the villagers gathered around and formed a huge group right in front of the village. Steve shouted:

- "Hello, everyone! My name is Steve; I'm the one who is going to defeat the dragon. Could you please take me to your leader and priest so he can help me in my quest?"

The villagers grabbed Steve by the hands and dragged him through the village. We followed them and they took us to a small house with a tower in the middle of the village. After arriving, the villagers left. Steve smiled at us:

- "Okay guys, this is it! Let's meet this priest now."

Day 25

It was a long trip. It took us almost two days non-stop to get here. And it was awesome to finally meet up with the priest who would help Steve with his quest. The priest was inside a small house in the middle of the village.

Steve hesitated for a moment, but then he opened the door. Next to a window in a corner, the priest was staring outside.

- "Come on in, please!" he said out loud.

Steve entered the house first, and we followed him.

- "I'm glad to see you here. Steve, right?"

- "Yes, sir! It's nice to meet you too. But how do you know my name?"

- "I've heard of you, Steve. The entire village has already heard of you. You're famous for being the only creature in this world that can control blocks and create new objects out of thin air. Your construction abilities are outstanding, and you're able to defeat monsters easily with powerful weapons and enchantments."

- "Well, that's one way to put it haha. Good to know! So you're aware of my visit, you know why I'm here, right?"

- "Yes, Steve. I know why you are here. You want to know how to reach the dragon, and how to defeat it, correct?"

- "Yes, that's what I want! Do you have that information?"

- "I do. In fact, it's all written in my book. I'll give it to you. But, there's one thing I'd like to ask you in exchange."

- "Sure, anything you want!"

- "Please stay in our village for 2 more days. We need your help with a specific matter."

Steve agreed to the condition.

Day 26

After spending a normal day at the village, we weren't sure as to why the priest asked Steve to stay there for 2 nights. Why did he need him?

We woke up in the next morning with the priest calling for Steve. He got up and talked with the priest:

- "Good morning, sir! So, do you need any help?"

- "Yes, in fact, I do. I asked you to stay here because we need your amazing skills. Tonight, we'll have a full moon, which means the Zombie Horde will attack our village."

- "Zombie Horde? I didn't know they could come in groups!"

- "They do, once every full moon. They're guided by a terrible leader, and they always try to invade our houses and take our food. That's why I asked you to stay here, because we need someone to build a defensive system and to fight the monsters."

- "It's the least I could do for all your knowledge and help, sir! Leave it to me and my wolves. We'll take care of those creatures!"

Yeah Steve, you can count on us! I was sure Oopa and I could help him defeat the Zombies.

- "I have a great idea of what to build. Leave it to me, sir; I'll start working right now!" Steve said. He left the house and started gathering materials such as wood and stone.

It was amazing to see Steve working. He was very fast, and he could destroy and place any blocks he wanted. The villagers were very impressed, as well. He crafted many tools to assist him in his job, and went off to chop down some trees. He also got a lot of ores and minerals.

The first thing he did was to dig a big hole around the entire village.

- "That's a very clever idea, Steve! He's making a moat, just like the ones in castles." Oopa said.

After making a deep hole, he filled it up with water using many buckets. Next, he made a small bridge to serve as the entrance. But this bridge was quite unusual… It would go up and down with the press of a button!

- "What kind of sorcery is that?" I asked Oopa.

- "It's a bridge made with Pistons. Those things are used to create automated systems!"

After finishing the moat and the bridge, Steve started building a huge wall: 4 blocks tall, made of rock. He built it in a few minutes.

- "Phew, we're done here! Now we just get ready to face the monsters if they trespass over the wall by any chance," said Steve.

Day 27

Steve worked a lot to prepare the village against the Zombie attack. The priest examined the work and was happy to see the big walls and the moat. As the night approached, the villagers entered their houses, and we followed Steve to the main entrance of the village. The priest was there, waiting for us.

- "Thank you for your help, Steve. I'm sure you'll be able to hold off against the horde."

- "No problem, sir. Now please go inside, for your own safety."

The priest left. It was past midnight. The full moon was very bright, shining over the village like a big spotlight. Everything was quiet. Suddenly, we saw something moving in the horizon. Oopa started barking. Steve grabbed his sword and pressed the button to close the bridge. The big shadow was getting closer, and from a narrow hole in the wall we saw it: a huge horde of zombies!

There were at least 20 or more in that first wave. They rushed in our direction. When they approached the village, they jumped in the moat, but apparently they knew how to swim.

- "Get ready, boys, they're coming for us!"

Fortunately the Zombies were slowed down by the water, and only a few of them reached the front gate. They started bashing the gate, trying to take it down.

- "The gate won't stand it any longer. We'll have to deal with them!" Steve said.

- "Take the ones from the right, and I'll cover the left, Boris!" Oopa said.

- "Okay, let's do this!"

The gate was taken down. Four Zombies invaded the village. Steve attacked 2 of them with his sword, and defeated them quickly. I jumped on one more zombie and Oopa got the other who was left.

- "Nice job, boys! Let's keep it up."

The zombies continued to cross the moat and tried to get inside the village, but we stopped them in the front gate. One by one, we defeated the 20 creatures, and Steve rebuilt the bridge after slaying the last beast.

Day 28

After rebuilding the bridge, we went back inside. It was very late and we were all tired. After having a nice night of sleep, we woke up with the entire village right in front of the priest's house. They were cheering and clapping, happy to see that the Zombie Horde was gone.

The priest came and handed Steve a small book.

- "I have no words to describe right now how happy I am for your help. Thank you kindly, Steve. Please take this book; it contains all the information you need to defeat the dragon and where to find it."

- "Thanks a lot sir! My pleasure. It was not hard at all to defeat the Horde with my loyal wolves by my side!" Steve happily smiled at us.

- "Steve, may I ask you something else?" The priest asked.

- "Sure!"

- "I know it's not part of our agreement, but... Could you please return here next month during the full moon again? You see, that Horde you defeated yesterday was just one of the many Hordes controlled by the Zombie Leader. I'm sure he won't be happy to know his Horde was defeated, and I believe his next attack will be much stronger. He might even come in person to make sure his Hordes get the job done."

- "Oh really? Glad to know that, sir. Because I wouldn't refuse to fight against them by any means! Don't worry; I'll be back here with my buddies to send those creatures back to where they belong."

- "Thank you again. You're always welcome in our humble village. Have a safe trip!"

Day 29

We need to get back home soon, so Steve can start working on his plans to defeat the dragon. He said he'll have to study the book and prepare his tactics very carefully in order to succeed. Fighting the dragon won't be easy, and Steve must be ready for it!

We spent the night in the woods, and we're not far from our castle now.

Day 30

After a few more hours travelling, we got home. Susi was outside, playing with the kids. We were all so happy to see each other! I hugged my kids and kissed Susi. They were also very happy to see Oopa and Steve, and we had a very nice feast.

Oopa and I told them the whole story, and since we're returning there next month, we'll be able to take everyone with us because the kids will be more than ready to take the road and help us against the next Horde.

Steve is reading the book right now, planning his strategy against the dragon. Oopa is playing with my kids, and teaching them a few basic attacks. We'll have to start training them for the battle against the Horde next month.

We have many challenges ahead of us, with strong and powerful enemies to defeat. But I'm sure we'll overcome those problems if we work as a team. And with Steve by our side, nothing can stop us!

ABOUT THE AUTHOR

Mark Mulle is a passionate Minecraft gamer who writes game guides, short stories, and novels about the Minecraft universe. He has been exploring, building, and fighting in the game ever since its launch, and he often uses in-game experiences for inspiration on creating the best fiction for fellow fans of the game. He works as a professional writer and splits his time between gaming, reading, and storytelling, three hobbies and lifelong passions that he attributes to a love of roleplaying, a pursuit of challenging new perspectives, and a visceral enjoyment the vast worlds that imagination has to offer. His favorite thing to do, after a long day of creating worlds both on and off the online gaming community, is to relax with his dog, Herobrine, and to unwind with a good book. His favorite authors include Stephen King, Richard A. Knaak, George R. R. Martin, and R. A. Salvatore, whose fantasy works he grew up reading or is currently reading. Just like in Minecraft, Mark always strives to level up, so to speak, so that he can improve his skills and continue to surprise his audience. He prefers to play massive multiplayer online games but often spends time in those games fighting monsters one on one and going solo against the toughest mobs and bosses he can manage to topple. In every game, his signature character build is a male who focuses mostly on crafting weapons and enchanting, and in every battle, he always brings a one hander sword and a shield with as much magical attributes as he can pour into them. Because he always plays alone, he likes to use his game guides to share all the secrets and knowledge he gains, and who know—he may have snuck some information into his fiction as well. Keep an eye out for his next book!

Made in the USA
San Bernardino, CA
30 April 2017